Dear Parent:

Congratulations! Your child is taking the first steps on an exciting journey. The destination? Independent reading!

STEP INTO READING® will help your child get there. The program offers five steps to reading success. Each step includes fun stories and colorful art. There are also Step into Reading Sticker Books, Step into Reading Math Readers, Step into Reading Phonics Readers, Step into Reading Write-In Readers, and Step into Reading Phonics Boxed Sets—a complete literacy program with something to interest every child.

Learning to Read, Step by Step!

Ready to Read   Preschool–Kindergarten
• **big type and easy words** • **rhyme and rhythm** • **picture clues**
For children who know the alphabet and are eager to begin reading.

Reading with Help   Preschool–Grade 1
• **basic vocabulary** • **short sentences** • **simple stories**
For children who recognize familiar words and sound out new words with help.

Reading on Your Own   Grades 1–3
• **engaging characters** • **easy-to-follow plots** • **popular topics**
For children who are ready to read on their own.

Reading Paragraphs   Grades 2–3
• **challenging vocabulary** • **short paragraphs** • **exciting stories**
For newly independent readers who read simple sentences with confidence.

Ready for Chapters   Grades 2–4
• **chapters** • **longer paragraphs** • **full-color art**
For children who want to take the plunge into chapter books but still like colorful pictures.

STEP INTO READING® is designed to give every child a successful reading experience. The grade levels are only guides. Children can progress through the steps at their own speed, developing confidence in their reading, no matter what their grade.

Remember, a lifetime love of reading starts with a single step!

For Lorie Ann Grover
—J.H.

To all the budding ballerinas everywhere
—S.M.

ISBN 978-0-545-68477-4

Text copyright © 2012 by Joan Holub.
Cover art and interior illustrations copyright © 2012 by Shelagh McNicholas.
All rights reserved. Published by Scholastic Inc., 557 Broadway, New York, NY 10012, by arrangement with Random House Children's Books, a division of Random House, Inc. Step into Reading is a registered trademark of Random House, Inc. SCHOLASTIC and associated logos are trademarks and/or registered trademarks of Scholastic Inc.

12 11 10 9 8 7 6 5 4 3 2 1   14 15 16 17 18 19/0

Printed in the U.S.A.   132

This edition first printing, January 2014

Ballet Stars

A STICKER BOOK

by Joan Holub

illustrated by Shelagh McNicholas

SCHOLASTIC INC.

Ballet show today— hooray!

We all dress up
a fancy way.

Sparkly ribbons.

Ballet shoes.

Bright white tights.

And new tutus.

We do stretches.

We do bends.

We warm up
with ballet friends.

Ballet arms.

Ballet feet.

Toes point out

and fingers meet.

Here we go
across the floor.

We run three steps,
then jump on <u>four.</u>

Look who's come
to see our show!

Our families and
some friends we know.

The music starts.

We find our places.

Happy smiles
on all our faces.

Twirl like snowflakes.

Sway like trees.

Dancing steps
in twos and threes.

Ballet dancers
in two rows
do ballet turns
on tippy-toes.

We bow to the left.

Blow kisses right.

We are ballet stars
tonight!